Monster Mess

Written by Tasha Pym
Illustrated by Olivia Villet

Collins

We painted spots.

We painted stripes.

We painted squares.

We painted zigzags.

9

We painted triangles.

We painted ... Mum!

Monster Mess

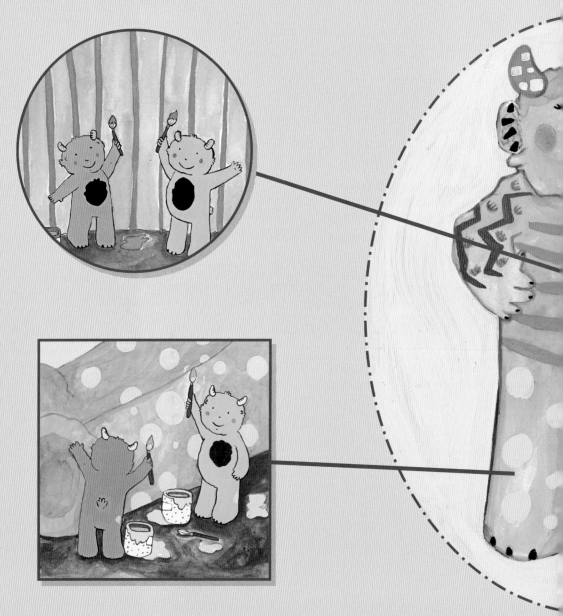

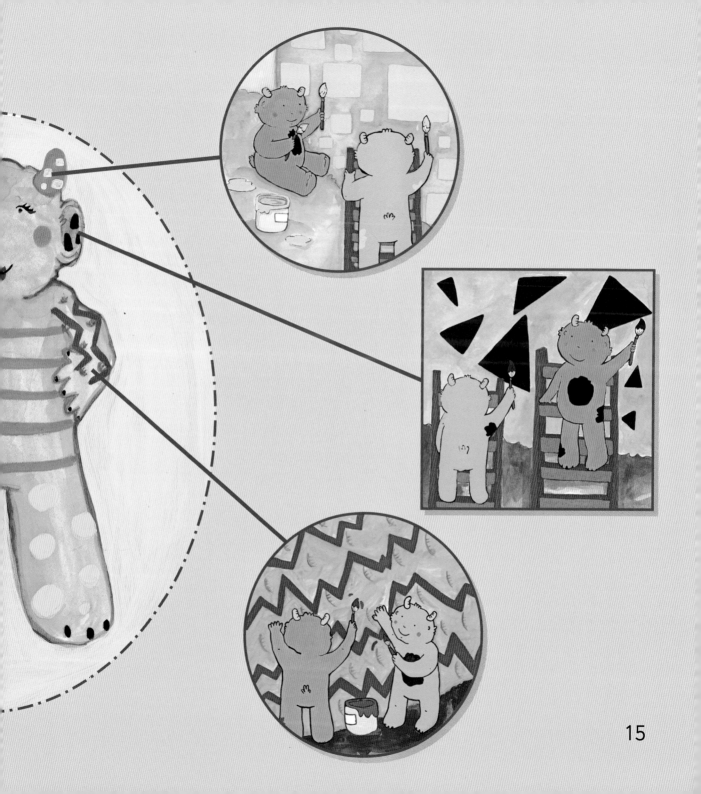

15

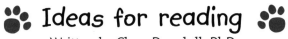

Ideas for reading

Written by Clare Dowdall, PhD
Lecturer and Primary Literacy Consultant

Reading objectives:
- use phonic knowledge to decode regular words and read them aloud accurately
- read and understand simple sentences
- demonstrate understanding when talking with others about what they have read

Communication and language objectives:
- follow instructions involving several ideas or actions
- listen to stories, accurately anticipating key events and respond to what they hear with relevant comments, questions or actions
- develop their own narratives and explanations by connecting ideas or events
- listen attentively in a range of situations

Curriculum links: Creative Development; Mathematical Development; Knowledge and Understanding of the World

High frequency words: are, but, like, little, mum, they, to, two, we, what

Interest words: monsters, painted, spots, stripes, squares, zigzags, triangles

Word count: 18

Resources: computer

Build a context for reading

- Look around the room for examples of different shapes: zigzags, stripes, squares, triangles.

- Ask the children to name as many other shapes as they can.

- Look at the front cover together and describe what is happening in the picture. What equipment, colours and shapes can the children see?

- Read the title together. Model sounding out the words *monster mess*. Ask children to stretch the word *m-o-n-s-t-er* to make as many sounds as possible.

- Read the blurb on the back cover together. Ask the children to predict what the monsters are painting in the story.

Understand and apply reading strategies

- Read pp1-3 together. Use your finger to point to the word that is being read.

- Encourage children to sound out the word *s-p-o-t-s* and to use the picture to make meaning.